THE HOSTEL

AN EROTIC ADVENTURE

VICTORIA RUSH

VOLUME 29

JADE'S EROTIC ADVENTURES - BOOK 29

COPYRIGHT

FEEL THE RUSH:

Jade's Erotic Adventures – Book 1

When lonely divorcée Jade seeks to broaden her horizons, she's invited to a private dinner event which promises to stimulate all of her senses. Wearing nothing but masquerade masks, dinner guests receive special service under the table while their fellow diners look on...

The Dinner Party

Jade's Erotic Adventures - Book 2

Jade discovers an exotic adventure club where strangers meet to explore each other's bodies in mysterious dark rooms. Using special effects to project swirling light patterns onto their figures, the shifting shadows provide just enough illumination to highlight their naked bodies while protecting their identities...

The Dark Room

Jade's Erotic Adventures - Book 3

Jade discovers a yoga club where members stretch and explore each other's bodies in the buff. She books an appointment, and during the first session meets a young redhead who tantalizes her with her flexibility and stunning body...

Naked Yoga

For the uninhibited...

SPICY ADVANCE EXCERPT:

A few minutes later, I smelled her familiar scent as she entered the darkened room. But instead of climbing the ladder to her own bunk, she lay down beside me, spooning me from behind. I lay still for a moment, unsure if she had amorous intentions or if she was just too drunk to climb the ladder. Either way, I was excited feeling her curvy figure next to me as goose bumps spread all over my body. When she reached around and cupped one of my breasts and softly squeezed my nipple, I turned my face toward her and we kissed quietly in the dark.

She pressed her tongue between my lips and we moaned softly, then I turned around to face her, feeling her naked breasts pressing against mine. Caught up in the passion of the moment, I wrapped my legs around hers, grinding my mound against her hairy pubis. I reached around the back of her ass and slipped my fingers down her crack toward her steaming slit. When I pressed the tips of my fingers into her opening, she groaned softly then rolled over on top of me.

Pulling my right leg up toward my chest, she reached down with her hand and plunged three fingers deep into my snatch. I grunted into her mouth, tilting my hips forward to meet her advance as I rolled her firm nipples between my fingers and my pussy sloshed quietly in the darkness. I wanted to feel her sex against mine, but I was so thrilled that she'd been bold enough to climb into my bunk without an invitation that I let her have her way with me while we kissed passionately.

As I grunted and gasped trying to contain the feeling of rising passion engulfing my body, it didn't take long for me to approach the crest of my pleasure. I pulled her face hard against me, moaning loudly into her mouth as my pussy clamped down over her fingers, squirting my juices all over her hand. Maria seemed startled by my show of waterworks and when I finished coming, she thrust both of my knees forward and positioned her thighs overtop of mine, lowering her dripping pussy onto mine...

1

———

I'd been looking forward to this trip for weeks. Besides the fact that it would be the longest vacation I'd ever taken, I'd created an open itinerary that allowed me to travel anywhere I wanted on my own schedule. I hoped to visit as many European countries as I could during my planned three weeks and stay as long or as little as I wanted based on how much I enjoyed each location. I wanted to be a free spirit, soaking up the culture of each place I visited, and let my experiences lead me from one destination to the next, rather than following a predetermined agenda.

I hadn't even booked a rental car or any hotels. Instead, I planned to stay at local hostels, crashing at whatever place was available wherever I went, experiencing the nomadic lifestyle of other wayward travelers. I'd be traveling alone and I heard that this was a great way to meet international travelers from different countries and make new friends. It was definitely taking me out of my comfort zone, accustomed as I was to having a plan and enjoying the luxuries of upscale hotels. But approaching my mid-thirties, I figured this was my last chance to take advantage of my dwindling youth while I still had the nerve.

My first stop was Rome, and when my Alitalia flight landed at Leonardo da Vinci airport late Friday afternoon, I hailed a cab and drove to the first hostel that came up on my Google search. When I checked in, I was pleasantly surprised with how clean and tidy the place looked. After paying for two night's accommodation, the clerk stowed my baggage and showed me around the facility. My dorm room was appointed with six single bunk beds arranged end-over-end on three walls of a ten-foot-square common room. It was smaller than I expected, but I hadn't come to Europe to sleep in the lap of luxury. I planned to be out most of the day, exploring the sights of the city and meeting new people.

There were two communal washrooms, a full-service kitchen, and a common terrace overlooking the pretty white-washed townhouses of the Trastevere District. It was hotter than I expected this late in the day, so after changing into linen shorts and sandals, I headed up to the terrace to meet some of my fellow travelers. After grabbing an espresso from the kitchen, I walked out onto the patio and was immediately invited to a table shared by five other overnighters.

"Buonasera!" a boisterous young man called out to me. "Come join us. We're all one happy family here."

I nodded my head and walked over to the table, taking the one vacant chair.

"I'm Diego from Barcelona," he said, reaching out his hand in greeting. "What brings you to Roma?"

"Jade, from Chicago," I said, clasping his hand firmly. "It's my first time to Italy. I figured I'd start with the biggest city and work my way north."

"Sounds like a good plan. How many days will you be staying in town?"

"I don't really have a set schedule. I thought I'd just go with the flow. You know, live in the moment, and all that."

"That's the only way to live," he said, raising a glass of wine and clinking it against my coffee mug. "Say hello to my friends."

I peered around the table as each traveler introduced themselves one at a time.

"I'm Tori, from Melbourne," a pretty blonde said, raising her glass.

"Ali, from Istanbul," a handsome young man with long dark hair said.

"Isabel from Cape Town," a cute freckle-faced girl said, smiling at me.

"Maria from Sao Paolo," an ebony beauty said, raising her glass of Prosecco.

"Wow," I said. "Talk about a worldly group. I think we've got every continent covered between us. I take it you're not traveling together?"

"What would be the fun in that?" Diego said. "Only old people and married couples travel in groups."

"Well I probably qualify as an old person compared to all of *you*," I chuckled, surveying the group of young faces.

"Are you married?" Diego asked.

"Not anymore."

"Well then you're not dead yet!" Ali said, raising his glass as everybody laughed.

"You're only as old as you *behave* anyway," Maria said, scowling at Ali for putting me on the spot. "The fact that you're traveling alone and staying at a youth hostel tells us you're young at heart."

"Thank you," I said, happy for the diversion. "How about you guys? How long are you staying in Rome?"

"Taking it one day at a time," Tori said. "Like you said, living in the moment."

"Amen to that," I said, lifting my cup. "Have you been here long? Where's a good place to start?"

"There's so much to see in Rome," Isabel said. "You can pretty much get off at any Metro stop and spend the whole day exploring any given neighborhood."

"The Metro?" I said. "Is that the city's public transit system?"

"Yes," Maria nodded. "It goes everywhere worth seeing. You can hitch a ride and follow along with us if you want to get your feet wet."

"I think I'd like that," I said, feeling my panties already beginning to moisten thinking about exploring the city with these pretty gypsies.

The six of us chatted well past midnight, sharing our travel experiences and backgrounds. Most of the group were university students taking the summer off to backpack around Europe. Besides me, Tori was the only one who was taking time off work. But she'd grown so accustomed to staying at hostels during her previous excursions, this was still her go-to mode of lodging.

Every one of the young travelers had a certain charm and allure, but there was something about Maria that I found particularly captivating. With her golden-brown skin, smoldering eyes, and puffy lips, she reminded me of a young Penelope Cruz. I could see her long, tanned legs through the porous surface of the wrought-iron tabletop, and it took every ounce of my willpower to keep my gaze focused on her face as I squeezed my thighs together trying to quiet my tingling clit.

By the time one a.m. rolled around, we'd all had enough Prosecco that we were laughing and teasing each other about our individual accents and cultures. As much as I would have liked to stay up all night commiserating with my newfound friends, I was beginning to feel the effects of jet-lag, and I was the first to turn in for the evening.

"You're probably going to think I'm acting like one of those old people," I said, getting up to excuse myself. "But I'm the only one who took a ten-hour flight today. I got up before dawn this morning and if I'm going to keep up with you guys while we explore Rome tomorrow, I need to get my beauty sleep."

"We'll give you a pass on your first day," Diego nodded. "But you're going to have to get used to this continental life-style. We Europeans stay up later and get up later than you obsessive-compulsive Americans. As the old saying goes—when in Rome, do as the Romans do."

"Give me a day or two to adjust my internal time clock, and I'll be happy to party all night long," I said. "But right now, I need to crash."

"Good night, pretty Jade!" Maria said, blowing me a kiss. "We're looking forward to having you join our group tomorrow."

As I staggered to my room from the combined effects of too much wine and too little sleep, I barely had the presence of mind to pull off my shorts and shoes, flopping into my lower bunk wearing only my panties. I fell asleep almost immediately, but sometime later, I was awoken by the sound of my dorm mates loudly entering the room and climbing into their respective beds. It was too dark for me to see who was sleeping in each bunk, but as I listened to someone climbing the ladder at the head of my bed to ascend into the bunk above mine, I smelled the distinctive aroma of a woman's perfume. I hadn't been able to place each person's individual scent on the outdoor terrace, but in the confined space of our small dorm room, it was quite distinct.

And *stimulating*.

There was something about being cooped up with a bunch of strangers in a communal space that got my juices going. We were so close to one another that we could hear each other breathing, and I lay awake for quite a while listening to everyone until they began snoring. But the person above me seemed to be unusually quiet, as if she was lying awake like me. I wasn't sure if it was because she couldn't sleep or if she also felt aroused by the close proximity of our bunkmates.

For the longest time, I lay perfectly still, trying to figure out who'd taken the bunk above mine. But when I heard her sheets begin to rustle and the bed frame begin to shake softly, I held my breath, darting my eyes in the darkness. As her breathing began to increase in urgency, it became obvious that she was masturbating in the darkness. Fearful about drawing attention to myself, I continued to lay still, listening to her pleasuring herself.

As the shaking of the bed grew progressively faster and her breathing became more labored, I slipped my fingers under my panties and began circling my clit, growing increasingly aroused listening to the girl above me. My mind drifted between the images of each person at the table, trying to guess which of the pretty girls it was. Each of them was attractive in her own right and I could have fucked any one of them, but it was Maria whom I fantasized about as I caressed my wet slit.

I imagined lying next to her in the darkness, feeling her warm body pressed against mine as we touched each other in our private areas, trying to stifle our moans as the rest of the room slept peacefully nearby. Suddenly, I wished the configuration of the sleeping quarters had been arranged with double beds instead of single bunks. I would have loved to crawl in next to her and kiss her while we pleasured each other quietly in the dark.

But the close separation of our beds only added to the sexual tension, as I listened to her juices smacking while she tribbed her wet slit with her fingers. I held my breath trying to hear every drip and sigh, feeling my own pleasure rapidly rising within me. When the girl suddenly squeaked and the bed frame began trembling, I knew that she'd reached her climax and within seconds I was biting my own lip trying to stifle my moans as I clamped my thighs tightly around my fingers over my convulsing pussy.

Even after I came down from my powerful orgasm, my heart was still pounding in my chest from the excitement of participating in our taboo act. I had no idea who it was who'd been pleasuring herself only inches above me or what had incited her impromptu fit of passion, but something told me this was only going to be the start of my little travel adventure.

2

———

The following day, the six of us hopped on the Metro train to explore Rome's historic city center. When we emerged onto the Piazza Barberini, I marveled at the beautiful buildings and sculptures styled in the classical architecture of the Eternal City. Everything gleamed in travertine marble, white-washed limestone, and orange-hued terracotta clay.

I gawked like a star-struck tourist gazing up at the large circular opening in the dome of the Pantheon while we took selfies standing in the bright beam of sun that slowly revolved around the interior of the ancient temple. Then we sat in the stands of the crumbling Colosseum, imagining ourselves watching a gladiator battle or a fast-pitched chariot race. And we gazed out from the tall granite columns of the Roman Forum, pretending to hold court over the passing citizens like the Roman senators and emperors of old.

By late afternoon, we were all exhausted from walking all day, so we stopped at an outdoor cafe to rest and get a bite to eat.

"There's so much to see in this city," I said, flopping into a chair and taking a sip of chilled San Pellegrino. "It seems like at every turn there's another amazing sculpture or building where you can linger for hours."

"And everything is so *old*," Tori nodded. "I can't believe some of these structures have stood for over two thousand years."

"That's because you're from the *new* world," Diego said, ordering a large pitcher of sangria for the table. "Australia and America were only settled a few hundred years ago, but parts of Europe and Asia have enjoyed an advanced civilization for thousands of years."

"It's a shame the Roman empire crumbled along with so many of its monuments," I said, making a subtle dig at Diego's veiled criticism of our two countries.

"But didn't America use the Roman model for designing its political institutions and many of its government buildings?" he said.

"I suppose so," I said. "Insofar as their both being a republic with a division of the executive and legislative branches of government. Unlike a *parliamentary* democracy, where the governing party can pretty much do whatever it pleases."

"Typical American," Diego said, taking a swig of sangria. "Thinking your country is better than the rest of the world."

"*Hey!*" Maria said, leaning forward to provide a barrier between the two of us. "We didn't travel from the four corners of the world to debate *politics*. Each of our countries has its own charms and limitations. We could do well to learn from the example set by this vibrant city. We're all just citizens of the world, after all."

"*Serefe*," Ali, said, raising his glass in agreement.

"*Prost*," Isabel nodded.

"*Zivoli*," Tori said, adding to the sentiment.

"*Saude*," Maria said, lifting her glass along with the others. Then she peered over at Diego and me still sulking with our arms crossed over our chests. "Did you know it's considered rude not to join in whenever someone offers a toast? And that if you don't look them in their eyes when you do it, that you could be sentenced to seven years of bad sex?"

"I had no idea," Diego chuckled, raising his glass and smiling at me. "*Salud*, to my new friends and world travelers!"

"*Cheers*," I said, peering at each of the handsome crew. "God forbid we'd all be cursed with seven years of bad sex!"

We ordered three large pizzas, and for the next hour shared more stories about our world travels and our plans for the future. But by the time we finished eating, the overhead sun had begun baking us to a crisp.

"I'll tell you *one* thing the Italians know how to do better than us Americans," I said. "That's how to make a good authentic pizza. Now I know what they're really supposed to taste like!"

"Amen to that," Isabel said. "But one thing I'm not digging about this place is how hot it gets at this time of the day. I don't know about you guys, but I could go for a dip in one of those Roman baths right about now."

"Unfortunately, all the public baths have long since been drained," Ali said. "Now they're just big stone pits we can only fantasize about. Besides, I'm pretty sure the Carabiniri frown upon tourists frolicking in their hallowed monuments."

"What about the outdoor *fountains*?" Tori said, pointing over to the nearby Fountain of the Naiads with its famous naked nymphs.

"I've heard that if the cops catch you so much as dipping your toes in any of the fountains that they'll fine you two hundred Euros," Diego frowned.

"Only if they *catch* us," Maria said, raising a playful eyebrow. "Come on, let's go have a little fun. Like you said, Diego, when in Rome..."

We all peered at one another for a moment, then placed some bills on the table to pay for our lunch and raced over to the fountain. When we got there, we flipped off our sandals and pulled off our shirts then jumped in the water, bouncing up and down holding hands. Maria was the only one of the girls who'd gone braless, and as the water splashed over her naked chest, I gazed at her pretty tits and flaring nipples.

But when the Italian police tweeted their whistles and began running toward us, we quickly gathered up our clothes, darting off in different directions from the circular piazza. When we saw that the coast was clear, we texted each other and regrouped at the closest Metro station, laughing as we hugged each other in our wet clothes. When we got back to our hostel, we changed into fresh clothes then met on the terrace for another late-night round of Prosecco and Espresso.

After talking into the wee hours of the morning, we staggered back to our bunks one at a time after making a quick pit stop in the communal bathroom. By the time I got into bed, everybody was already fast asleep, snoring all around me. But once again, the sound from the bunk above me was strangely quiet. Not sure if Maria had turned in ahead of me, I listened quietly for any sign of movement.

A few minutes later, I smelled her familiar scent as she entered the darkened room. But instead of climbing the ladder to her bunk, she lay down beside me, spooning me from behind. I lay still for a moment, unsure if she had amorous intentions or if she was just too drunk to climb the ladder. Either way, I was excited feeling her curvy figure next to me as goose bumps spread all over my body. When she reached around and cupped one of my breasts and softly squeezed my nipple, I turned my face toward her and we kissed quietly in the dark.

She pressed her tongue between my lips and we moaned softly, then I turned around to face her, feeling her naked breasts pressing against mine. Caught up in the passion of the moment, I wrapped my legs around hers, grinding my mound against her hairy pubis. I reached around the back of her ass and slipped my fingers down her crack toward her steaming slit. When I pressed the tips of my fingers into her opening, she groaned softly then rolled over on top of me.

Pulling my right leg up toward my chest, she reached down with her hand and plunged three fingers deep into my snatch. I grunted into her mouth, tilting my hips forward to meet her advance as I rolled her firm nipples between my fingers and my pussy sloshed quietly in the darkness. I wanted to feel her sex against mine, but I was so thrilled that she'd been bold enough to climb into my bunk without an invitation that I let her have her way with me while we kissed passionately.

As I grunted and gasped trying to contain the feeling of rising passion engulfing my body, it didn't take long for me to approach the crest of my pleasure. I pulled her face hard against me, moaning loudly into her mouth as my pussy clamped down over her fingers, squirting my juices all over her hand. Maria seemed startled by my show of waterworks and when I finished coming, she thrust both of my knees forward and positioned her thighs overtop of mine, lowering her dripping pussy onto mine.

When I felt her lips meld into mine, I wrapped my arms around her back, pulling her down on top of me. As she began rocking her hips, our pussies began making wet smacking sounds in the dark while we hummed and flicked our tongues together. The feeling of her hot vulva rubbing against mine was sublime and as we ground our clits together, I could feel her hips moving with increasing intensity as she neared her climax. When it finally washed over her, the two of us clutched each other tightly, grunting into each other's mouths in a powerful simultaneous climax. Trying to stifle our noise, we lay locked together in a tight kiss as we listened to each other's heavy breathing.

Suddenly, I became aware of the stark silence filling our darkened dorm room, sensing that the rest of my bunkmates were no longer sleeping soundly. Within seconds, we both heard the telltale sounds of rustling sheets and beds rhythmically squeaking all around us. Apparently, the sound of our lovemaking had woken everybody up, arousing them to their own heights of passion. As soft moans and sighs began filling the room, Maria lifted her head above mine and smiled at me.

Neither one of us had said a word the entire time she'd lain next to me. We didn't have to–the sounds of passion everywhere around us told us everything we needed to know.

3

———

When I woke up the next morning, Maria was no longer lying beside me, so I went to the washroom to relieve myself then grabbed a coffee and headed up to the terrace where the rest of the group was already assembled. As I approached the table, everyone looked at me with a knowing smile except Maria, who was peering out onto the esplanade, pretending like nothing had happened.

"Buongiorno, sleepyhead!" Isabel said, pulling out a chair for me. "How did you sleep last night?"

"It was a pretty late night," I said, avoiding Maria's gaze. "I could have used an extra couple of hours to keep up with you guys."

"I dunno," Diego said, sitting back in his chair as he took a sip of espresso. "From the sounds of things in the room, it looks like you're doing a pretty good job keeping up with the rest of us."

"How do you mean?" I said, shaking my head.

"Come on," he said. "Was I the only one who heard the

squeaky bed and the sound of obvious lovemaking coming from Jade's bunk?"

Everybody peered at me and smiled.

"The only question is, who *joined* you in your bed after we all fell asleep? It was so dark in the room it was impossible to tell. And when I woke up in the morning, everybody was nestled back in their individual beds."

"*Diego*," Tori said, peering at him disapprovingly. "What everybody chooses to do in the privacy of their own bedroom is their business. Stop picking on Jade!"

"Except it's not really *her* bedroom, is it? We share it as a group, so it kind of *is* all of our business."

"Well I don't know about you guys," Maria said, trying to deflect attention away from me. "But her bed wasn't the *only* one squeaking last night. Whatever was going on in our room, it sounded to me like *everybody* was enjoying themselves."

"Fair enough," Diego said. "That was pretty hot, you have to admit. I think we *all* got pretty worked up listening to whoever was getting it on in the dark."

"Maybe you lifted that bad sex curse after all," Ali laughed, raising his cup of coffee.

"So it would seem," Diego said. "But with six attractive people crammed together in a small room, stuff is bound to happen. I mean, prior to that you could have cut the sexual tension with a knife. Swimming in the fountain half-naked, getting sloshed on Prosecco late at night, then literally sleeping on top of one another in the dark. Don't tell me I'm the *only* one who's feeling it?"

Everyone sipped their coffees silently, shifting uncomfortably in their chairs.

"I have an idea, if you guys are open to a having some fun," Diego said. "Since the room is too dark at night to know who's pairing up with whom, why don't we make a little game of it?"

"What did you have in mind?" Isabel said sitting up, obviously intrigued by the Spaniard's proposal.

"Why don't we draw lots to encourage some more exploration? Whoever draws the same lot number has to meet in a designated bunk that particular night. Because it will be random, none of us will know who's hooking up with who."

"What if we don't *like* who we're hooked up with?" Maria said.

"Or if the gender pairings don't fit with our sexual preferences?" Ali frowned.

"Nobody's forcing anybody to do anything," Diego said. "If you don't feel like having sex or you're uncomfortable with your chosen partner, you can just shrug it off and go your separate ways. What do you think? Or are we just going to continue sneaking around in the dark and pretend like nothing's happening?"

Everybody sat quietly at the table for a while, pondering Diego's idea. Then Tori was the first to break the silence.

"How will we know which bed to go to if it's all going to be random?"

"We'll designate one communal bed," Diego nodded. "Let's say Jade's, for the sake of argument. It's on the lower level and wedged between the other two rows, so that's the best place for the rest of us to listen in. Those who aren't selected can choose whatever other bed is empty."

"You mean we won't be sleeping in our same beds each night?" Isabel said.

"That would make it too easy to know who's hooking up with who. Half of the fun will be guessing who's using the lower bunk each night. We might have to pay a little more to have fresh sheets replaced every night, but that shouldn't be a problem."

"So how will this work exactly?" Ali asked. "Will we draw straws or something to see who has the shortest ones?"

"We could do that," Diego said, peering around the table for something to use. "How about if we just write six numbers on separate pieces of paper and designate two of them to be the appointed pairing for that evening?"

He picked up a menu card from the table and tore it into six pieces, then scribbled a number on the back of each one. Then he folded the slips over so we couldn't see the numbers and threw them in a bowl.

"Okay, let's each draw one slip of paper from the bowl. Whoever draws number four and six have to join up tonight. But don't tell anyone what number you've drawn. You won't know until later tonight who you'll be sleeping with."

"Maybe we'll *never* know," Isabel smiled. "There's four girls and two boys. It could be pretty much *any* combination and in the pitch dark, it might be impossible to tell who you're partnered with."

"Unless it's the two *dudes*," Ali said. "That combination will be pretty obvious right away."

"But like Diego said," Maria smiled. "Half of the fun is in not knowing who you'll be paired with. If you don't tell, we'll never know. The more we talk about this idea, the more I like it."

"Okay," Diego nodded. "It's settled then. If this works out as well as we expect, we can draw new lots every night until we leave."

"That's *one* way to get to know each better," I smiled, disappointed to see that the number I'd chosen wasn't one of the indicated ones. But I couldn't be too unhappy. After all, it was my secret rendezvous with Maria that had kicked this whole thing off.

———

We decided to explore the Vatican that day, and for the next few hours nobody made any further mention of Diego's daring plan.

Walking up the broad avenue leading into St. Peter's Square, we gazed at the large colonnaded plaza with the ornate sculptures of one hundred saints peering down on the visiting crowd. In the center of the square lay a tall Egyptian obelisk installed by the emperor Caligula in AD 39. As we climbed on the pedestal for a group photo, I wondered what the famously randy monarch would think of our kinky plan to spread the love amongst our group of wayward travelers.

When we entered the huge basilica at the head of the plaza, we played a fun game of Marco Polo, calling out each other's names while we pretended to hide in the many porticos and side chambers of the cavernous church. Our next stop was the Sistine Chapel, where we lay on the marble floor gazing up at the colorful frescos painted on the ceiling by the famous artist Michelangelo. With so many naked figures touching and fondling one another in the busy illustration, my pussy tingled imagining who'd be hooking up tonight in our dark dorm room.

Then we walked through the Vatican museums, housing some of the most beautiful and expensive pieces of sculpture and paintings anywhere in the world. In the Pinacoteca painting gallery, the resplendent artworks were arranged in chronological order from the Middle Ages to the 1800s. And the Museo Pio Clementino's collection of ancient sculptures rivaled that of any public museum. As we walked past the oversize casts of nude men and women, we fondled their exposed genitalia when the guards weren't looking, giggling like little kids. By the time we reached the ornate sculpture gardens behind St. Peter's Basilica, I was so horny I wanted to duck behind one of the trees to rub a quick one out.

But when we finally got back to the hostel, it was already three a.m., and instead of heading up to the terrace for our customary late-night drink, we all stumbled into our sleeping quarters. After turning out the light and closing the door, we felt our way to the nearest side bunks, climbing into bed alone. But we all knew that two designated people from our group would be sleeping together in my old bunk.

While we lay breathlessly waiting in our individual beds, it didn't take long to hear the telltale sighs and moans of two women caressing each other in the lower bunk. As I began to circle my tingling clit, my mind began wondering which of the three girls had been paired together, and I felt a pang of jealousy wondering if Maria was sharing her magnificent body with someone else.

As the bed began to squeak and shake with increasing intensity, I tried to imagine what position they'd entangled themselves into in the small enclosed space of the lower bunk. I could hear the dripping sound of moist pussies being caressed, and I wasn't sure if they were touching each other with their fingers, mouths, or vulvas. Thrusting my fingers into my dripping cunt, I began fantasizing about the various things I planned to do when my turn hopefully came around again.

As the girls grunted and groaned with increasing urgency, I began to hear sighs and moans emanating from the other bunks. I smiled at the genius of Diego's outlandish idea, and as much as his arrogant attitude sometimes annoyed me, I was happy everybody had gotten on board with it so quickly. When I heard a head bump against the top of the lower bunk, I knew the girls were no longer just lying beside one another. It was obvious that one of them had assumed the superior position and was humping her body against her partner. Whether she was sitting on her face or rubbing another part of her body wasn't clear. Either way, the imagery was driving me crazy with desire as I visualized the two women grinding their bodies against one another.

But when I heard the sound of their voices rising in tandem, I knew that they'd joined together as the sound of wet pussies rubbing and smacking filled the cabin. Within a few minutes, the entire room was filled with the sound of all six of us climaxing one after the other. When the cacophony finally died down, soft giggling rose from the lower bunk when the girls realized how much they'd aroused the passions of the rest of the group listening in quietly from their private beds.

I had a hard time falling asleep that night fantasizing about the different combinations of partners that might find themselves joined together over the next few nights. Suddenly, my open-ended travel agenda where I'd planned to visit many other European countries had changed. I was no longer in a hurry to leave Rome and move on to my next destination.

4

W hen I woke up the next morning, everybody was still sound asleep in their bunks, so I had a quick shower and headed up to the terrace to have a peaceful cup of coffee. Before I left the room, I noticed Tori was sleeping in my old bed with Isabel in the bunk above her. Maria was the first to join me on the terrace, followed by the other two girls. We didn't make any mention of the previous night's activity, but when Diego and Ali approached the table, they peered at us inquisitively.

"Isn't this convenient that the four *women* were the first to get up this morning," Diego smiled, taking a seat next to us. "*Now* how are we supposed to figure out who was having all the fun in the lower bunk last night?"

"Like you said," Maria smiled. "Half the fun is not knowing who's pairing up. Besides, I thought we were supposed to keep it a secret."

"Can you at least tell us if *you* guys know?" he asked, taking a sip of his coffee. "I mean, *somebody* had to have seen who was sleeping in the lower bunk when you got up."

"Who's to say she wasn't the first one to get up?" I said.

"Then the *next* person to wake would have seen her outside the room."

"You're trying far too hard to figure it out," Isabel chuckled.

"It sounded like he was trying pretty *hard* to figure it out last night, too," Tori teased. "At least judging by all the deep moaning. From the sound of things, you guys seemed to have enjoyed the experience almost as much as the designated couple."

Diego crossed his leg as a slight flush fell over his face.

"Who knew it could be so much fun listening to two people making out?" he said.

"So, what's the plan for tonight?" Ali said. "I'm kind of itching for my turn."

"I guess we do the same thing as last time," Diego said. "We'll all draw lots again and see who picks the lucky numbers."

"But if we do that, there's a good chance someone who's already participated will be chosen *again*, which reduces the chances for the rest of us," Ali said.

"And how can we draw random lots without revealing who's already had their turn?" Isabel asked.

Diego paused for a moment while he thought about how to make it work while still preserving everybody's privacy.

"Okay," he said. "How about this idea? We'll all draw random numbers like before and designate two of them to be tonight's pairing. But if someone who's already participated chooses one of those numbers, then we'll select two back-up numbers. In the unlikely event those have also been taken, we'll choose two more."

"What about the couple from the night *before*?" I asked, hoping to get back in on the action. "Are they also excluded?"

"It seems only fair," Diego nodded. "Just to make sure everybody gets his turn."

I darted my eyes from side to side doing the math, then a big smile formed on my lips. Knowing that Maria and I were the first to pair up and that Isabel and Tori had their turn last night, that only left Diego and Ali.

"Okay, I guess that makes sense," I said, hoping to execute the plan before Diego changed his mind. "But I don't know if management is going to appreciate our ripping up their menu again."

"Never fear," Diego said, pulling a notepad and a pen out of his pocket. "I came prepared this time."

He ripped a page off the pad then tore the paper into six small pieces. Then he scribbled separate numbers onto each slip, folded them in half, and threw them in the empty bowl on the table. We all reached in and grabbed one of the slips and leaned back, viewing our selected number.

"Right, let's make this as simple as possible," Diego said. "If you've chosen numbers one and two and you haven't already hooked up, then it will be your turn tonight. But if you have, then we'll move to number three, then four if you've *both* already had a turn. In the unlikely event that the first four numbers will have already been used, then it will be numbers five and six who'll hook up tonight."

Unlikely indeed, I smiled, realizing that Diego's strategy had unwittingly forced the two men into the same bed tonight.

We decided to take a river cruise down the Tiber River that day, followed by an open-air picnic in one of Rome's biggest parks, then wrap up the night partying at a local nightclub. The more time we spent together, the closer we grew together as a group, switching spots on the riverboat whenever we hopped on and off at stops along the way. By the time we reached the end of the cruise, I'd learned much more about each of my new friends. When we exited the boat at its southern terminus, we spread out a large blanket on the lawn of Parco De Medici, then we laughed and played frisbee until we fell asleep in a jumble on the grass.

After having a late dinner at a restaurant overlooking the river, we headed to the nearest nightclub and danced past midnight. Watching everybody bumping and grinding their bodies together on the dance floor got me pretty worked up, but I was particularly excited watching Diego and Ali playfully bump their asses together, knowing what was in store for them later that night.

When we got back to the hostel, everybody was already buzzed from drinking all night long, and we staggered back to our room, tearing off our clothes and heading to our individual bunks. Everybody except *Diego and Ali*, who collapsed into the lower middle bunk, still not realizing that the odds had been stacked against them from the start.

The sheets rustled for a few moments and it didn't take long for the two men to realize they'd been paired together. There was a long pause, then the rustling resumed as soft breathing sounds began emanating from the lower bunk. I'd intentionally picked the bunk above them to have a better listening angle, but at first it was difficult to decipher what they were doing. Then I nodded when I heard the distinctive sound of lips smacking and popping like someone was licking a lollypop. It was obvious that one of the men was sucking the other one's cock.

I smiled, suddenly feeling aroused picturing the two

men touching each other intimately. I'd always found the idea of two men making love to be a huge turn on, and as I listened to the moaning and humming noises beneath me, I rolled my erect nipples between my fingers wondering who was sucking who. As a slapping sound slowly began to fill the chamber, I could hear the sound of one of the men's moaning growing louder. I wondered if his partner was stroking his shaft simultaneously, slapping his balls against his ass.

Yes, I grunted, rubbing my wet pussy with the palm of my hand as I listened to the two men.

But as fast as the moaning and slapping sounds had risen, they stopped just as suddenly. I heard somebody whispering, then the men shifted position in the bed and the fapping sound resumed with a different sounding moan. Within seconds, I heard the lollypop sound again and I knew that they'd switched positions, with the other one now receiving his first boy-on-boy blowjob.

Whether their inhibitions had been loosened by the alcohol we'd been drinking or from all the bumping and grinding on the dance floor was unclear. All I knew was that I was enjoying the sound of the two straight men sucking each other's cocks, and from the soft sighs and rustling sheets coming from the *other* three beds, so were the other women.

While I lay on my back with my legs spread wide, I jilled my clit listening to the sound of their masculine moans below. As before, the pace and intensity of the smacking sounds continued growing in intensity, and I was sure this time that the one on the receiving end would soon blow his load. But just as things seem to reach the point of no return, the rustling sounds suddenly stopped and one of the men whispered something.

"Wait," I heard him murmur. "I don't want to come too fast. Why don't we try doing this *together*?"

I couldn't tell right away that it was Diego's voice, but his bossy attitude made it obvious who was talking.

"You mean like *sixty-nine*?" Ali whispered back softly.

"No, I was thinking we could rub our cocks together instead," Diego replied. "Cross your knees and sit in front of me."

The two men shuffled their position in the bed, then one of them bumped his head against the upper deck.

"Fuck!" Ali yelped.

"Be careful, man," Diego said.

"*Uhnn*," Ali suddenly groaned when the shuffling stopped. "That feels awesome. I can feel your cock throbbing against me."

"Yeah man," Diego said. "Rub your cock against mine. You're dripping all over me."

I heard some more shuffling sounds, then both men moaned as they began moving their bodies together in unison. ·

"Fuck yeah," Diego panted. "Wrap your hands around our dicks while we rub them together. This feels amazing."

I heard the sound of their sticky precum mingling as they rubbed their dicks together in the dark, then one of them spit overtop of their joined cocks, trying to provide better lubrication. They grunted for a while, then I heard some more spitting as they tried to gain better traction. Having given enough hand jobs in my previous marriage, I knew from experience how lousy pre-cum acted as a lubricant. Reaching beside me, I grabbed the tube of lube I'd brought with me into the bed and reached over the side, dropping it on the bed below me.

"Try *this* stuff," I whispered. "I think you'll find it makes a better lubricant."

There was a pause as the two men weren't sure how to respond, then I heard the lid pop open as someone squirted a dollop of lube on top of their joined cocks. Within seconds, a different, more *slippery* sound began to fill the cabin as the lower bunk began to rumble from the combined action of the two men rubbing their cocks together.

"Fuck *me*," Diego hissed. "This is so much better. Are you feeling it too?"

"Yeah," Ali panted. "I can feel your balls rubbing up against mine. Grip our cocks harder. I'm going to come soon."

"Yeah, man," Diego panted. "I want to feel you cum all over my chest."

"*Fuck* yeah," Ali panted, nearing the crest of his pleasure.

Suddenly the shaking and panting sounds stopped as the men stopped moving again.

"What are you *stopping* for?" Diego hissed. "I was just about ready to come!"

"I was thinking we could try something else before we pop off. I'm enjoying this too much to stop so quickly. After we come, we'll be too soft to do anything else."

"What did you have in mind?" Diego said.

I heard a soft rustling sound as Ali whispered something in Diego's ear.

"I don't know, man," Diego said. "I've never done anything like that before. I'm not gay."

"Neither am I," Ali said. "But haven't you ever done it with a girl and wondered what it would feel like to try it with a guy?"

"Not until *now*," Diego replied. "I'm so fucking horny I could fuck just about anything right now."

"Now that we've got some proper lube," Ali said. "Turn over, then I'll let you do me after I finish."

"Okay," Diego said. "Just be careful with that thing. I don't know how much of you I'll be able to take."

"No worries, man. Just let me know if I'm hurting you."

I heard Diego flip over onto his stomach as Ali kneeled beside his upturned ass. Then he squirted the lube, spreading the gel over Diego's crack. Ali hesitated with his erection positioned over Diego's sphincter, then he moaned as he sunk into his hole.

"*Fuckk*," he groaned. "You're so tight. Does it hurt?"

"No," Diego said. "Just go slow. It's not as bad as I thought it would be."

"*Uhnn*," Ali grunted as he pressed his length inside his Diego's rectum. "This is nothing like fucking a woman's pussy. It's so much tighter and hotter."

"Yeah, fuck my ass, man," Diego said. "Put it all the way inside me. I can feel your cock massaging my prostate. *Damn*, that feels good."

Suddenly, the bed frame shook as Ali plunged his cock all the way inside Diego's ass. For a short moment, he paused reveling in the feeling of his cock embedded inside an unfamiliar sheath, then he began to ram his hips against Diego's ass as he began fucking him hard from behind.

"Are you sure it's okay?" Ali said, no longer trying to disguise his voice. "It doesn't hurt?"

"No," Diego panted. "Fuck my ass, man. Let me feel you come inside me."

"Yeah," Ali grunted with increasing urgency. "It's going to happen soon, man. My balls are so tight. I can feel your slippery ass rubbing up against me."

"I feel them too," Diego said, tilting his hips higher into the air to meet Ali's thrusts. "Come for me, man. Let me feel your dick throbbing inside my ass."

"Oh God," Ali groaned. "Here it comes, man. I'm going to come."

"Do it man," Diego grunted along with his partner. "This is so fucking hot."

Suddenly, the bed shook violently as Ali thrust his hips one last time hard up against Diego's ass, depositing his cream deep inside his bowels.

"*Unghh*," Ali hissed, holding himself balls-deep against Diego's backside.

Up to that point I'd been paying so much attention listening to the sounds of the two men fucking each other that I hadn't realized the other *women* were enjoying the show almost as much as them. When Ali began grunting in the throes of a powerful orgasm, the other girls began moaning along with him as the smacking sounds of their dripping pussies filled the cabin. There was a long pause while Ali finished pumping his seed into Diego's ass, then I heard some more shuffling sounds as the two men began to uncouple.

"Fuck, man," Diego said. "That was amazing. I had no idea how much fun that would be."

"Wait until you try it on *top*," Ali said. "I haven't come that hard in years. Do you want to give it a try?"

"*Fuck* yes," Diego hissed. "Turn over. I'm going to fuck your ass like it's never been fucked before."

The bed squeaked as the men switched positions, then I heard the tube of lube squirting as Diego emptied its contents all over Ali's waiting pucker.

"Fuck, man," Diego panted. "I'm so fucking hard, it hurts."

"Put it in me," Ali said. "I want to feel you inside me."

I heard Diego grab Ali's buttocks and spread them apart, then he positioned his dick at the opening to his hole and thrust his cock deep inside Ali with one powerful thrust.

"*Uhnn!*" Ali grunted, not expecting such a forceful maneuver.

"Sorry, man," Diego said. "Are you okay?"

"Yeah," Ali rasped. "I just didn't realize how big you were until you put it inside me. Fuck my ass. I want to feel your balls slapping against my butt cheeks."

Holy shit, I thought, listening to the two men talking dirty to one another. This was even sexier than I'd imagined. As I listened to the sound of the bunk squeaking beneath me while both men groaned, I thrust my fingers deep into my cunt, fucking myself wildly.

"Holy fuck!" Diego hissed, ramming his dick in and out of Ali's back door. "You weren't kidding about how tight this is."

"Yeah," Ali said. "Is it as good as fucking a woman?"

"Maybe *better*," Diego said. "There's something about doing it with a guy that's kind of dangerous that makes it even more arousing."

"Yeah, man," Ali said. "Slap your balls against my ass. I want to feel you dump your load inside me."

With the sound of slapping skin filling the cabin, my mind raced with the imagery of the two men connected in carnal pleasure. As Diego's breathing began to escalate toward his inevitable climax, I began to feel the telltale sensation of my own climax rapidly approaching.

"Oh *fuck*," Diego moaned. "I can feel it in my balls. I'm going to come, man. Holy shit, I'm going to come in your ass. *Ngahh!*"

As Diego rammed his pole deep into Ali's cavity,

emptying his load into his bowels, my pussy clamped down hard over my fingers, gushing my juices all over my hand. With the sound of multiple orgasms suddenly filling the darkened room all around me, I smiled at how far I'd come during my short visit to Italy. I'd never imagined becoming so enmeshed in intimate relations so quickly with a bunch of strangers, and as we all flopped back onto our mattresses exhausted after a long day of sexual build up, I wondered what would be in store for us next.

5
____

There wasn't much need for second-guessing the following morning, since everybody knew who'd been using the lower bunk the previous night. After sleeping in late, we all crawled out of bed and headed up to the terrace with coffees in hand.

"So how did *you* two sleep last night?" Maria said to Ali and Diego as we all sat down together at our communal table.

"Um, pretty good," Diego said, pretending like nothing unusual had happened.

"I *bet* you did," she smiled. "It sounded like you had a pretty good workout before you nodded off."

"It was *that* obvious, was it?"

"Are you *kidding* me? That was the most entertaining sex show I've heard in a long time."

"How long did it take you to figure out that it was the two of us?" Ali said.

"Like about *two seconds*," Maria said. "You guys were pretty vocal."

"I guess we kind of got lost in the moment," Diego said.

"That's not the *only* thing you apparently got lost in," I said, winking at Ali.

"So what happens now that we've all had a turn in the lower bunk?" Isabel said, giving the boys a break from our playful cross-examination. "Do we choose more numbers to see if we can mix up the combinations?"

"I was thinking about that," Diego said, leaning back in his chair. "I know some of us will be moving on to our next destination tomorrow. Why don't we make it a little more interesting by putting *three* of us together tonight? We still haven't had a boy-girl match-up yet, and by adding one more person to the mix, we increase our chances of getting both sexes involved."

"Are you sure you *want* to?" Tori said, arching an eyebrow toward Diego. "You guys seemed to enjoy your same-sex match-up pretty fine last night."

"We were just playing the game like the rest of you," he said. "We didn't want to be killjoys by interrupting the flow. I can't speak for my friend, but I still prefer girls."

"*Definitely*," Ali nodded, peering over the rim of his coffee cup.

"Since we've all had a turn, we'll pick three numbers this time. Whichever three chooses those numbers will join up in the lower bunk tonight."

"That could be a bit of a tight squeeze in the narrow space of a single bed," Tori frowned.

"I guess we'll just have to find a way to *layer* ourselves then," Diego said with a wry smile.

"What about the *other* three?" I said. "Do we just sit by and *listen* again?"

"I think we all know each other pretty well enough by now," Diego said. "I don't see any reason why the rest of the group should just sit idly by. I would encourage you to hook up however the mood strikes you. The more the merrier."

"I'll tell you *one* thing," Isabel said, leaning back in her chair. "This has certainly been the most *stimulating* trip I've had in a long time."

"Cheers to that," I said, raising my cup.

As everybody raised their cup and joined in the toast, we all laughed out loud.

For our final day together as a group, we decided to go to a nude beach. It was only a thirty-minute bus ride to the west coast of the peninsula, and we sang old hippie songs as we thrust our arms out the open windows, waving at the passing tourists. When we got to Capocotta Beach on the Mediterranean, we stripped off all our clothes and ran into the warm surf, hugging and chasing each other through the rolling waves.

This was the first time I'd actually seen any of them fully naked, and I soaked up each of their dripping bodies with wide eyes. They all had lean, youthful figures, and with the distraction of the beckoning sea, I had plenty of time to ogle their physiques. As expected, Maria was the curviest of the women, with large, buoyant breasts and a Jennifer Lopez shaped ass. My pussy tingled under the lapping waves as I remembered what it felt like having her rub up against me three nights ago, and I hoped I'd have another chance to hook up with her before we all went our separate ways.

But the other two girls were just as sexy in their own way. Tori's long wet hair draped over her perky tits, accentuating her long, pointy nipples. With her golden-brown tanned skin and large blue eyes, she looked like a classic

Sports Illustrated swimsuit model. And Isabel's fair skin glistened in the overhead sunshine, illuminating her beautiful naked body like a porcelain doll.

But it was the *boys* who I had the hardest time keeping my gaze diverted from. Both Ali and Diego had slender and ripped figures with a thick coating of dark hair covering their carved pecs and washboard stomachs. Both of them were nicely equipped below, and as they jumped up and down in the roiling surf, I stared at their pendulous peckers flapping up and down over their tight ballsacks. As much as I preferred to have sex with other women, it was always a nice treat bringing a man into the mix once in a while.

We picnicked on the beach, then played an impromptu game of volleyball, laughing while we got all covered in sand. When it was finally time to leave the beach, we toasted to our last sunset over Rome before heading back to our hostel. Although I hadn't picked one of the winning numbers for tonight's meet-up, I had my *own* plans for making my last night in Italy memorable.

After enjoying a late-night round of amaretto, we all headed to the dorm room together and switched off the light, closing the door softly behind us. As we all groped our way to the nearest bunks, I chose one of the lower beds and waited for the action to unfold. When I heard two girls and a man laughing in the middle bunk, I smiled, happy to hear that Diego's plan had finally mixed both genders together. Not long after, I felt the familiar shape of a woman's naked body climb in next to me, and I turned to kiss Maria on her lips.

"I'm glad I have you all to myself one last time," I whispered in her ear.

"There was no way I was going to let you leave without making love to you again," she purred.

Suddenly, we felt another pair of hands groping us from outside the bunk, and we turned to see who was invading our space.

"Have you guys got room for one more?" Diego whispered.

Maria and I peered at one another in the dark then squeezed our hands together playfully.

"What do you think, Jade?" she said. "Shall we bring one more into the mix to make it a little more interesting?"

"I suppose it wouldn't hurt," I said. "We don't want to leave poor Diego to his own devices for the rest of the night."

I shifted over to the edge of the wall to make room for him, and he slid in next to Maria, facing her face-to-face. She lifted one of her legs and he pressed his hips forward, poking his stiff phallus under her slit. I felt his dripping crown and massaged his head with my right hand while I reached around and squeezed Maria's tits with my other hand.

"*Somebody's* in the mood to play," I joked, flapping Diego's hard pole against Maria's vulva.

"I've wanted you two for myself from the moment I saw you," Diego panted, sucking Maria's fat nipples between his lips.

"I don't know what you were *waiting* for," Maria said. "We didn't need a game of chance to pull this off. We've been thrust together in this small space for quite a few days now."

"I didn't want to invade anyone's privacy," he said. "I wasn't exactly getting an *open signal* from you two up to now.

Maria wrapped her upper leg over his hip and tilted her pussy toward his dripping hard-on, placing the tip against her wet slit.

"How's *this* for an open signal?" she purred. "You can invade my space any time."

Diego didn't waste a moment angling his hard-on into her hole, slowly sinking his length inside her. I placed my hand around his shaft as he entered her, surprised at how long and thick his erection was. When he reached the end of her cavity, I grabbed his scrotum and squeezed his balls as he groaned loudly.

"*Fuck* me with that big python of yours," Maria panted, beginning to rock her hips in unison with him.

For a brief moment, I was jealous of Maria giving all of her attention to Diego, but as I listened to the two of them panting and groaning, I satisfied myself running my fingers over her curvy backside and feeling his balls flexing as he pounded his cock inside her. It didn't take long for the combined sensation of my stroking his undercarriage and Maria engulfing him with her wet pussy for him to begin panting with increasing excitement. I would have been happy to caress both of them while they convulsed in the throes of orgasm, but apparently Maria had other ideas. After a few minutes she stopped moving her hips, then backed away, pulling Diego's flaring cock out of her snatch.

"What's wrong?" he said, obviously frustrated with her last-minute withdrawal.

"Nothing," she purred. "I was just feeling sorry for Jade. Don't you think it's only fair we bring her in on the action?"

"*Absolutely*," Diego hissed. "A threesome is every man's dream."

"Do you mean having two *women* or another man with a woman?" she teased.

Diego paused as he listened to the sound of our other bunkmates groaning in the adjacent bunk.

"After last night, it could work either way," he said. "But something tells me that Ali is kind of preoccupied right now. How did you want to *do* this exactly?"

"Why don't you lie down on your back while Jade and I figure out what to do with you," she said.

"I like the sound of that," Diego said, rolling onto his back.

"Why don't you play with his outie part while I enjoy the innie part?" Maria said to me as I climbed on top of Diego's prone body.

"Okay," I said, smiling in the darkness. "I think I can find something to do with that."

I rubbed my wet vulva on Diego's hard stomach, then tilted my hips as I shifted my ass backwards until I felt the tip of his dripping pole probing my slit. I paused for a moment, teasing him by rocking my wet opening against his dick as he jerked his hips forward, desperately trying to penetrate me. Meanwhile, Maria turned around to face me and straddled his face with her hips, pressing her warm pussy down over his chin.

"Mmm," Maria purred, rolling her wet cunt all over his face. "I like the feel of your scratchy stubble on my soft skin. Would you like me to give you a little facial?"

"Hmm," Diego hummed, unable to talk with Maria's thighs clamped around his head.

"What about *you*, Jade?" Maria asked. "Are you ready to give Diego the ride of his life?"

"I think that can be arranged," I said, pushing my hips backwards a few more inches, pressing the tip of his burning prick into my hole.

"Mmm," Diego moaned, finally feeling his cock getting some much-needed direct friction.

"You *like* that, baby?" Maria said, leaning forward to squeeze my tits as I began to hump Diego's big dick.

"Uh-hmm," Diego nodded, still pinned under Maria's undulating hips.

We were both enjoying having total control over Diego as we slowly measured out our attention for him, getting back at him for his condescending comments earlier.

"That's it," she purred. "Suck on my clit like you were sucking Ali's cock last night. How's it working for you, Jade? Is he as big as Ali said he was?"

"It's not the *biggest* I've had," I joked, slowly pressed my hips further down his cock. "But it'll do in a pinch."

When I felt his balls pressing up against the back of my ass, I began rocking my hips and squeezing my walls against his rock-hard organ.

"What do you think, Diego?" I teased. "Am I as tight as a man's pussy? Do you think my cunny will do in a pinch?"

Diego moaned under the weight of Maria's hips, grabbing the side of my ass, pulling me harder against him. As he began to pound his dick deep inside my tunnel, Maria and I leaned forward intertwining our tongues while we pinched each other's nipples. As we listened to Diego getting more and more aroused from the sensation of two women squirming over his body, Maria pulled back and turned her face toward the side of my head.

"Shall we torture him a little longer?" she whispered into my ear.

"Absolutely," I said, mashing my tits against hers.

"Pull away for a sec," she purred. "I have an idea."

I pulled my dripping pussy off Diego's throbbing cock while Maria lifted her hips off his face, inching closer toward me.

"What the *hell*?" Diego said, still pinned under the weight of our two bodies. "Weren't you guys enjoying that? You're driving me *crazy*!"

"That's the idea," Maria purred, shifting her weight further down Diego's belly until her mound pressed against his upturned pole. "It's not fair that Jade gets to enjoy that big johnson of yours all by herself. What do you say, Jade? Are you willing to share some of that fresh meat?"

"My pleasure," I said, positioning my vulva against the underside of Diego's dripping pole.

"What about *you*, Diego?" she purred. "Would you like to get fucked by two women at once?"

"Yes please," he panted, vainly trying to move his dick between our two vulvas.

As Maria and I began rocking our hips together, rolling our wet slits up and down his pole, I could feel his precum dripping down the sides of his flagstaff, intermingling with our slippery juices.

"How do you like *this* kind of lube?" Maria said to Diego, trying vainly to reach up and squeeze her big tits from behind. "Is tribbing with two women's natural juices anywhere near as good as frotting cocks with a *man*?"

"Much *better*," Diego gasped, jerking his hips wildly against our joined hips. "This feels incredible."

I had to admit that I was enjoying our three-way trib as much as Diego, and as I leaned forward to kiss Maria on her lips, I moaned softly into her mouth as we writhed our pussies together over Diego's burning pole. While I listened to her moaning harder as she increased the speed of her hips rocking against the two of us, I wondered if she'd pull away to torment Diego one last time. Instead, she wrapped her arms around my back and held me close as she groaned loudly in my mouth, reaching the peak of her pleasure. When she dug her nails into my back and flapped her thighs wildly against mine in the throes of climax, I felt my own orgasm wash over me as I gushed my juices all over Diego's tight balls.

When he heard us coming and felt my juices dripping

down his crack, he grunted like a wild animal, erupting like a geyser all over Maria's and my breasts. As Maria and I held each other tightly, pressing our pussies together around Diego's throbbing member, we smiled listening to the sounds of passion coming from the adjacent bunk. Even though I'd barely set foot outside Rome for the bulk of my overseas trip, I felt like I'd been on a whole *different* kind of world tour staying holed up at my little hostel.

Spying on the neighbors just got a lot more interesting...

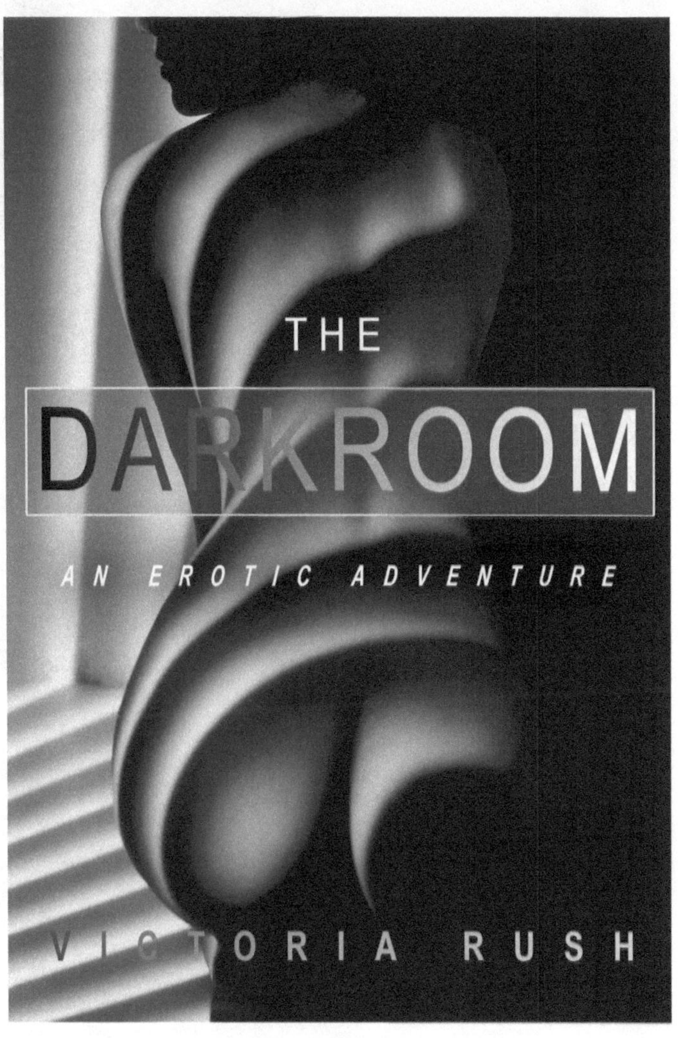

Everything's sexier in the dark...

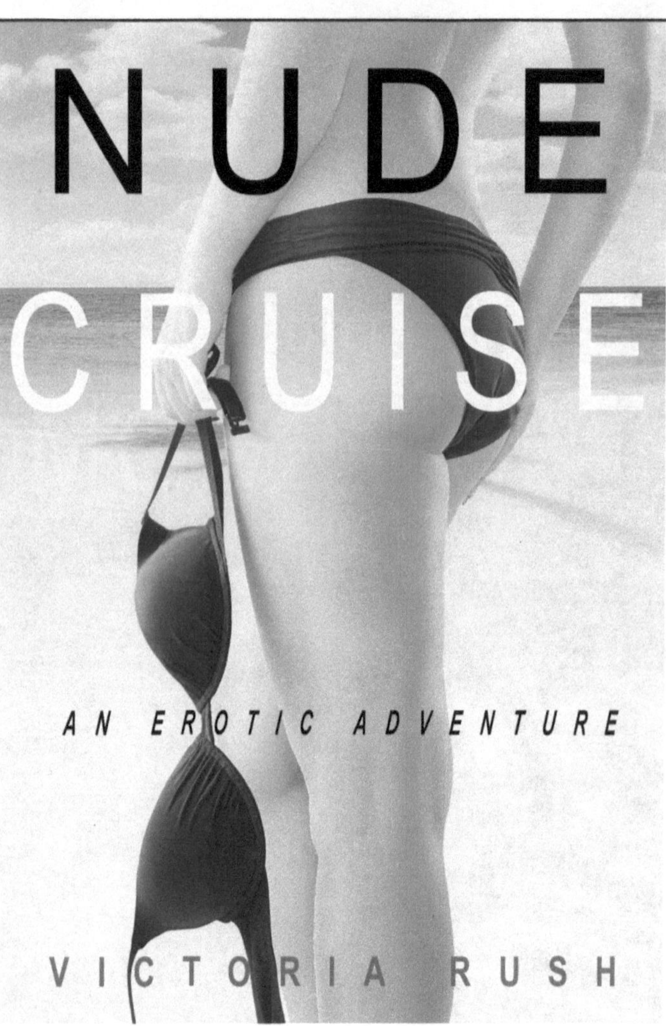

Some people get wet on a cruise for different reasons...

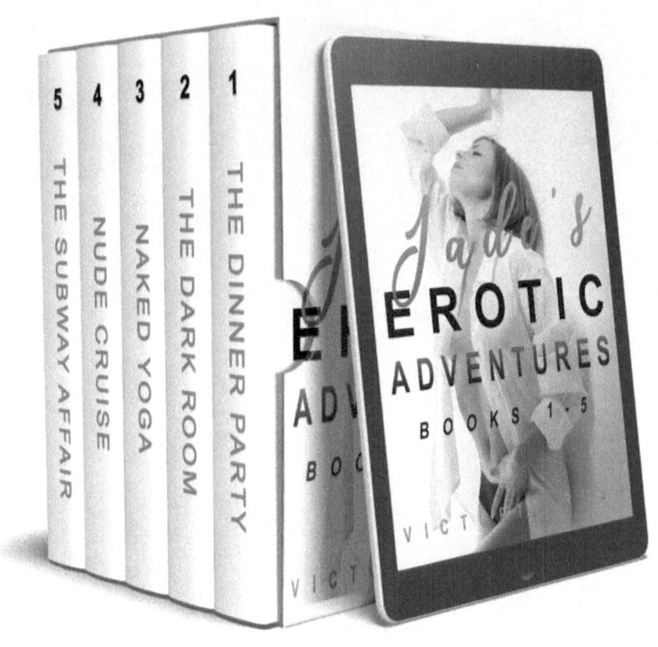

Books 1 -5 in the bestselling erotica series - 60% off

THE DARE - PREVIEW
CHAPTER 3

"Okay, so now that I'm committed, tell me where you had in mind for this little experiment."

"Actually," Hannah said, "I have a *series* of places in mind, each one more challenging than the one before."

"But I thought you said this was a one-off proposition?"

"I said nothing of the sort. I only said that if you won, I'd pay for the flights to Bora Bora. If you want me to cover the cost of hotels, food, and all the other incidentals, you'll have to pass progressively tougher tests. We don't want to make this *too* easy for you, do we?"

I crossed my arms and huffed, putting on my best pouty face.

"It hardly seems fair," I said. "But I'm still game. Besides, either one of us can pull out at any time to lock in our gains, right?"

"I suppose so," Hannah shrugged. "But what would be the fun in that? Something tells me once you've tried the first experiment, you won't want to stop. I think you're going to find this whole thing quite titillating and exciting. This will be the most fun either one of us has had in a long time."

I pushed the rest of my half-eaten salmon dish to the side, suddenly no longer interested in eating.

"Okay, lay it on me then. Where are you planning to take me for the first test?

Hannah gulped down the rest of her margarita then peered at me with a lopsided grin.

"Church. More specifically, a *Catholic* church. You haven't been in quite a while, have you? This will be your chance to repent and atone for all your sins."

"It's not like I've broken any commandments or anything–"

"The Catholic Church still considers sex outside of marriage a mortal sin. So technically, you've been doing a ton of sinning since your marriage ended."

"Well I haven't been a practicing Catholic for ages," I snorted. "So my conscience is clear. This'll be a cakewalk. All I have to do is sit quietly in my pew, right?"

"Yes, but it'll be a *front-row* pew, in full view of the priest who'll be delivering the sermon."

"Okay, but I'll be fully clothed, right? It's not like there'll be anything for him to see..."

"Not if you can keep your composure and don't cum all over the floor," Hannah said, cocking her head playfully.

"I don't think I'll have any difficulty keeping my dick in my pants, in a manner of speaking. But you raise a good point. You can't expect me not to get a little wet while you're stimulating me. What will I be allowed to wear?"

"I assume you'll dress appropriately, wearing your Sunday best. A mid-length skirt and button-up blouse should do the trick. You should be able to hide a few dribbles that way, right?"

"I suppose so, but how will we muffle the sound of the vibrator buzzing inside my panties? There's likely to be other people sitting around me in adjacent pews..."

"Never fear," Hannah smiled, reaching into her purse and pulling out a U-shaped silicone sex toy. "I've been talking with our friend at the local Babeland store. She's given me the latest prototype of the We-Vibe vibrator to test." She held up a smaller device with two control buttons and a flywheel. "Complete with a Bluetooth remote control. And the best thing is that it's whisper-quiet.

"Here," she said, handing me the flexible device. "See for yourself."

She tapped one of the buttons on the remote and the thick side of the contraption began buzzing softly in my hand.

"Okay," I nodded, looking around me to see if any other restaurant patrons were distracted by the gentle hum of the object. "It's *quiet* enough, but which end goes inside?"

"The bulbous end is a natural G-spot stimulator. You place the flatter end against your clit, then pull the thing up tight against your vulva to keep it snugly in place."

I suddenly became mindful of the wetness permeating my panties as I imagined the device vibrating inside me, surrounded by a bunch of oblivious bystanders.

"Can I give it a try here, like we did last time?" I grinned.

"No way," Hannah said, pulling the toy out of my hands. "There'll be no trial runs for this or any future tests. You'll just have to wait until we get to the church."

"And where will *you* be sitting while this is all going down?" I said.

"Right next to you, of course. I'll want a front-row seat to watch all the action."

On Sunday morning, Hannah picked me up and drove me the two miles to our local church. The entire time I squirmed in my seat trying to imagine what it would be like having a vibrator buzzing inside me in the quiet chapel. When we got to the church parking lot, she pulled into a sheltered space then plucked the blue vibrator out of her purse and handed it to me, resting her arm on the seat cushion expectantly.

"*What?*" I said. "You don't trust me to put it in privately?"

"Not really," she smirked. "For all I know, you might pull on some adult diapers under your skirt to hide any unintended releases. Here," she said, handing me a plastic vial. "I brought some lube to make it go in easier."

"I don't need any," I said, pulling the vibrator out of her hands and placing it under my skirt. "I'm already plenty worked up thinking about this scenario."

"I hope you're wearing panties under that skirt," Hannah said, watching me shift my weight as I placed the device against my vulva. "We wouldn't want it popping out at an inopportune moment."

"I'll just have to leave that up to your imagination," I sneered, lifting my skirt halfway up my thigh. "Unless you need to inspect the goods to make sure I'm not cheating."

"I trust you," Hannah smiled, opening her car door. "Something tells me you're looking forward to this just as much as I am."

As we approached the entrance to the church, I noticed a familiar figure standing at the top of the steps greeting the incoming parishioners, and he made eye contact with me when Hannah and I approached the landing.

"Jade!" Father Fife said, holding out his hands to me. "I haven't seen you in such a long time. It's so good to have you join us again."

"I'm sorry, Father," I said, placing my sweaty hand between his. "I've been a little distracted lately..."

"Life has a habit of getting in the way of the important things," he said. "We're just glad to have you whenever you can find time." He turned to Hannah, raising his eyebrows in curiosity. "And who's this lovely lady you've brought with you to attend our service today?"

"This is Hannah," I said, motioning toward my friend. "I thought I'd bring her along for moral support."

"Happy to have you, Hannah," Father Fife said, clasping Hannah's hands warmly. "The Lord knows we all need moral support wherever we can find it."

Hannah nodded politely, then the two of us walked through the entrance doors where I dipped my hand into the bowl of holy water and crossed my chest before continuing on toward the front of the chapel.

"*Jesus*," Hannah whispered, peering around the imposing shrine. "Is it just me, or did that feel a little creepy? All that talk about *having* us and that prolonged hand-holding. Hasn't he been paying any attention to the me-too movement?"

"I'm not sure any of that applies to men of the *cloth*," I chuckled. "But you better be careful about using the Lord's name like that around here. If anybody overhears you, you're liable to be burned at the stake."

The two of us stepped lively down the main aisle and finding a free spot in the front row, we took our seats flanked by two elderly couples. It was hard to imagine how Hannah would be able to use the remote-control device sandwiched so closely between other parishioners, and I crossed my legs, thankful for the brief respite. When everyone had filed into the chapel and the bell signaled the start of the service, a hush fell over the chamber and we all stood up as Father Fife walked onto the pulpit in his flowing robes.

"In the name of the Father, and of the Son, and of the Holy Spirit," he intoned solemnly.

"Amen," the congregation murmured in unison.

"The Lord be with you," he said.

"And with your spirit," the couples beside me retorted.

What the hell have I gotten myself into? I thought, feeling the flexible vibrator pressing against the inside of my closed legs. I didn't consider myself a terribly religious person, but being in this holy place surrounded by all the familiar rituals brought back all the old memories from my parents about the consequences of sinful behavior. *Surely getting secretly stimulated by a sex toy in the house of God will send me straight to hell.*

This was the point in the church service where everybody was supposed to take a moment to make a penitential act. While I listened to the other parishioners around me making their supplications, my knees began shaking as I made my own silent prayer for forgiveness.

"May Almighty God have mercy on us all," the priest said. "Forgive us our sins, and bring us to everlasting life."

"Amen," I joined in the congregation's response.

"Let us pray," Father Fife said, bowing his head.

As we closed our eyes and he began his opening prayer, Hannah nudged me with her knee and my mind raced with images of the pastor scornfully looking down at us while we played our blasphemous game. I peered up as he flapped his Bible closed, and caught him glancing in my direction.

"Through our Lord Jesus Christ, your Son," he said. "Who lives and reigns with you in the unity of the Holy Spirit, one God forever and ever."

"Amen," I said aloud, hoping he'd see me behaving like a good Catholic girl and turn his attention elsewhere.

He motioned for everyone to sit down and I was glad to get off my shaky feet onto the relative safety of the wooden pew.

"Good morning, ladies and gentlemen," he began his homily. "Today, I would like to talk with you about *morality*. Specifically, about the decaying state of society's morals in today's world. All around us we are surrounded by prurient symbols of modern decadence. First it was in the form of the printed word, then motion pictures, then the ubiquitous internet. It seems everywhere we turn, we are bombarded with profane and sacrilegious images."

I felt my heart pounding in my chest, like he was singling me out personally for my not-so-infrequent porn surfing.

"We seem to have forgotten," he railed, "the Lord's commandment that we shall not covet thy neighbor's wife. This admonition can be taken in its broadest context. Not only have many of you forsaken the sacred institution of marriage, but the egregious and widespread popularity of obscene *pornography* belies our unbridled lust and depravity. God slew Onan for spilling his seed, and so He will strike all others who practice self-abuse."

Hannah nudged her knee against mine, suddenly

reminding me why we were here. I was glad that she hadn't yet had the opportunity to take out her remote-control device, and I prayed that we'd be able to get through most of the service without her rudely interrupting it. I'd already begun to regret agreeing to this little venture, and I hoped that somehow we'd be able to bypass this first phase in her experiment.

"I'd like you to pick up your Bibles," Father Fife said, interrupting my thoughts. "And turn to Mark, Chapter 7, Verse 20."

Hannah and I reached down to pick up the bibles lying on the seat beside each of us, and we flipped to the indicated section.

"Read this passage with me, my friends," Father Fife instructed. "What comes *out* of a person is what defiles him," he enunciated, while the congregation quietly murmured along.

As I began to recite the passage along with him, I saw Hannah reach into her side pocket and place her closed hand between the book binding.

"For from within come evil thoughts," I continued reading as I peered out of the corner of my eye to see what she was up to.

"Sexual immorality, adultery, coveting, wickedness..." we read in unison.

Suddenly, I felt the interior end of the vibrator begin to tremble inside me and I stuttered, trying to finish the passage.

"Deceit...sensuality...envy..." I stammered, trying to catch my breath as I followed along. Hearing my labored recital, Hannah turned her head in my direction, acknowledging my silent suffering. She knew exactly what I was feeling and how difficult it was for me to remain composed as I read the script.

"All these evil things...come from *within*," I gulped as I began to feel the pleasure spread across my pelvic region. "And they defile a person."

"Consider these words carefully," the priest said, surveying my hunched-over posture. "For the Lord does not abide salacious thoughts and behavior. If you want passage into His Kingdom, you must be as pure and righteous as He."

He paused for a moment to let the message sink in, then he motioned with his two hands for us to be seated. I was grateful for the rest, and I froze upright in my chair trying to ignore the movement of the possessed instrument inside me.

"Let us consider for a moment *another* one of God's ten commandments," Father Fife continued. "Thou shall not commit *adultery*. The Lord made Eve from the flesh of Adam, and in so doing signified that forever more man shall be united to his wife as one..."

As Father Fife ramped up the intensity of his gayphobic critique, so did Hannah, furtively adjusting the flywheel on the remote-control device nestled under her palm in her lap. As she slowly increased the speed of the vibrations emanating inside my pussy, I squirmed on the bench, trying to restrain my rising passion.

"By rejecting the sanctity of marriage," Father Fife continued, glancing distractedly in my direction, "you have all *sinned*. In the book of Deuteronomy, we saw that God ordered adulterers be stoned to death. For your indiscriminate behavior, so shall the Lord indiscriminately smite thee."

Jesus, I thought. If that's what awaits a sinner for

cheating on their spouse, I wonder what happens to someone who self-abuses herself while sitting for Sunday Service in a house of God. *Surely I'll burn in hell for this act of sacrilege.*

Just when I thought I was beginning to get control over the delicious sensations stimulating my insides, Father Fife instructed us to stand once again and recite another passage from the Bible.

"Please stand now and read Peter 1:16 with me," he said.

Everyone stood and dutifully flipped to the relevant section of the scriptures. This time it was even harder for me to stand motionless, as my knees fluttered unsteadily from the pleasurable sensations radiating inside me.

"It is written..." I tried to read along. "That you shall be holy, for I am holy."

I saw Hannah's hands moving once again inside her prayer book, and suddenly I felt the *other* end of the U-shaped vibrator buzzing against my clit.

"And now Galatians 5:16," Father Fife instructed, barely giving me a chance to recover.

I flipped to the new citation and gasped for breath as my legs wobbled beneath me.

"But I say," I panted unsteadily. "Walk by the Spirit, and you will not gratify the desires of the flesh."

"So it is written," Father Fife said, closing his Bible. "Be righteous as the Lord, and you shall join him in Heaven for everlasting days. And now," he said, magnifying my torture. "I would like us to sing together one of my favorite hymns celebrating His blessing, *Amazing Grace.* Please pick up your hymn books and turn to page forty-three."

"Amazing grace, how sweet the sound," the priest began to sing as the entire congregation joined him in harmony.

"That saved a wretch like me," I sang along, trying to

ignore the message that seemed targeted directly at me. As I tried to hold the melody, Hannah cupped the remote-control device in her hand and turned the flywheel to its maximum setting.

"I once was lost, but now am found," I hyperventilated, pressing my legs together as hard as I could to stifle the rising passion that threatened to overtake me.

"Was blind, but now I see," I squealed, singing the last word decidedly off-pitch as Father Fife turned to see my entire body shaking as I belted the famous hymn.

By the time I'd finished the song, I'd somehow managed to keep it together and fight off the cresting passion that had threatened to put me over the edge. When we finally sat back down, Hannah mercifully turned the vibrator off, and I spread my hands over my ruffled skirt to signal that I'd managed to keep myself composed.

When the service was over and we walked up the aisle behind the rest of the assembly to exit the church, I couldn't wait to get out of the building to wash myself off, figuratively and literally. I was glad that we were at the back of the crowd so nobody could see the back of my skirt. I wasn't sure if my leaking pussy had left a stain, but I sure as hell didn't want one of the parishioners pointing it out. When we finally exited the entrance doors, Father Fife turned to the two of us and smiled.

"I noticed you seemed a little more passionate than usual reciting today's passages, Jade" he said to me.

"Yes, Father," I said, shaking his hand unsteadily. "I felt truly embodied by the spirit."

"And *you*, Hannah," he nodded. "Did you enjoy today's service also?"

"Oh yes," she said. "It was the most moving sermon I've attended in a long time."

"I hope you'll both come again," Father Fife said to the two of us.

"I'm sure we *will*, Father," Hannah smiled as we continued down the steps.

Like the second we get back home, I thought to myself, dying to tear off my clothes and squirt all over Hannah's face while she ate out my still-dripping pussy.

READ MORE...

ABOUT THE AUTHOR

If you would like to receive notification of new book(s) in Jade's Erotic Adventures, follow me at http://bookbub.com/authors/victoria-rush.

If you have a moment, please post a brief review on my Amazon book page at viewbook.at/thehostel . Even just a couple of sentences will help other readers find and enjoy this book as much as you hopefully did.

Follow, share, like, and comment at:

www.facebook.com/authorvictoriarush
www.pinterest.com/authorvictoriarush
www.twitter.com/authorvictoriarush
authorvictoriarush@outlook.com

Hope to see you again soon!